# Mad Iris Goes Missing

by

## Jeremy Strong

## Illustrated by Scoular Anderson

*You do not need to read this page – just get on with the book!*

First published in 2006 in Great Britain by
Barrington Stoke Ltd
www.barringtonstoke.co.uk

ISBN 1-842993-65-8

Printed in Great Britain by Bell & Bain Ltd

## Meet The Author – Jeremy Strong

*What is your favourite animal?*
**A cat**
*What is your favourite boy's name?*
**Magnus Pinchbottom**
*What is your favourite girl's name?*
**Wobbly Wendy**
*What is your favourite food?*
**Chicken Kiev (I love garlic)**
*What is your favourite music?*
**Soft**
*What is your favourite hobby?*
**Sleeping**

## Meet The Illustrator – Scoular Anderson

*What is your favourite animal?*
**Humorous dogs**
*What is your favourite boy's name?*
**Orlando**
*What is your favourite girl's name?*
**Esmerelda**
*What is your favourite food?*
**Garlicky, tomatoey pasta**
*What is your favourite music?*
**Big orchestras**
*What is your favourite hobby?*
**Long walks**

With my best wishes to Mad Iris and
her mad family in Athens

# Contents

# Chapter 1

# What has Happened to Mad Iris?

Not every school has an ostrich. That's what made Pudding Lane Primary a very special school – they *did* have an ostrich. It wasn't a pretend one. It wasn't a toy one or a stuffed one either. It was a real ostrich, and her name was Mad Iris.

Mad Iris had escaped from an ostrich farm. She ran as far away as she could.

1

When she stopped running, she found she was in the playground of Pudding Lane School. The teachers tried to chase her away, but the children liked Mad Iris because she ate their pencils and then they couldn't work. Mad Iris liked the children too, because she liked eating pencils. The children wanted her to stay.

Then the men from the ostrich farm came to get her. Ross and his friend Katie hid Mad Iris in the boys' toilets. Katie *says* she's Ross's girlfriend, but Ross says no, they're just ordinary friends. Who do you think is right?

The men found Mad Iris and Ross. They chased them onto the flat roof of the school. They were going to shoot Mad Iris, but Mr Grimble, the headteacher, stopped them. That was when the school decided that Mad Iris could stay. She became the school mascot.

If you're asking why Katie wasn't up on the roof with Ross and Mad Iris, I'll tell you. She had got her feet stuck down a toilet bowl. It took Mr Grimble and Ross a long time to get her out. That was after they'd come down off the roof. If you want to know more you'll have to read MAD IRIS, which is the first book about Mad Iris. This is the second.

Mad Iris lived in the caretaker's shed. The caretaker didn't think this was the right place for an ostrich, but he couldn't get rid of her. He had to find somewhere else to go, so he shared the cook's little office with her. He liked that, and the cook liked that and soon they got married – but that's another story.

Mad Iris liked the caretaker's old shed because it was full of interesting things that made interesting noises when she chewed them. They often had interesting tastes too. For example, she might eat a bit of rubber tube. It made squeaky noises in her beak and it tasted of ... well, it tasted of rubber, of course.

Another time, Mad Iris might eat a small pack of screws. Mad Iris didn't know if she liked eating screws. They were a bit hard to chew, but she liked the way they sparkled. She tried to eat the screwdriver too, because somehow it seemed to go with the screws. Mad Iris was certain she did *not* like the screwdriver. It was too pointy and sharp. She spat it out. Then she stamped on it and kicked it under a cupboard so she wouldn't have to think about it any more.

Everyone at Pudding Lane liked having an ostrich as their school mascot. No other school had anything like Mad Iris. Bottom End Primary had a fluffy pink teddy for their mascot. Top End Primary *said* they had a real shark for their mascot. They said they kept it in the school swimming pool. Nobody at Pudding Lane believed them of course, except the five-year-olds in Year One. But then most of the children in Year One also believed Mr Grimble had special super powers. He didn't.

So the children at Pudding Lane Primary were very happy, and so was Mad Iris.

But then, one morning, Ross and Katie and their friends went to say "Hello" to Mad Iris, like they did every morning before school. They opened the shed door and she wasn't there!

MAD IRIS HAD VANISHED!

# Chapter 2
# Ross Does some Thinking

"Where is she?" asked Katie.

"I don't know," snapped Ross. How should he know? He spotted a scrap of paper on the floor and picked it up. "It's a note," he said.

"What does it say?" asked Buster, one of Ross's friends.

"It says HA HA," Ross told them, looking puzzled.

"Ha ha?" repeated Katie. "What's that supposed to mean?"

Ross looked at her and frowned.
"I suppose it means HA HA, like in HA HA. How am I supposed to know what HA HA means? That's all it says."

"Someone is playing a trick on us," Katie growled, and Buster nodded.

"Do you think the teachers are having a joke?" he asked.

They went to see Mrs Norton, who was their class teacher. They told her that Mad Iris had vanished. Mrs Norton was very surprised and said she didn't know anything about it. Then they all went to see the head teacher, Mr Grimble.

Mr Grimble hurried to the empty shed and peered inside. "Oh dear," he muttered. "She must have escaped."

"She left a note," said Buster.

"Don't be silly!" said Ross. "Mad Iris can't write! Somebody else left the note, and that means somebody else was here." He showed Mr Grimble the scrap of paper.

"HA HA," read Mr Grimble. "Do you know what? I think Mad Iris has been kidnapped."

"Kidnapped?" echoed Ross and Katie. "Why would anyone want to kidnap an ostrich?"

"I don't know," said Mr Grimble, "but it's happened at the very worst time. We've got the football final against Top End Primary at the end of this week. They've won the cup every year so far. They always beat us in the final."

"That's because they cheat," said Katie. She was angry. Katie was one of the stars of the football team.

"Maybe they do," agreed Mr Grimble. "Even so, I was hoping we would beat them this year. I thought Mad Iris would bring us good luck. If she was watching we might win this year. It would be brilliant if we could beat Top End at last!"

Ross was looking down at the ground. He was thinking hard. He frowned a bit. Then he frowned a bit more and then he frowned a lot.

"What's up with you?" asked Buster.

"I've been thinking," said Ross. "It's odd that Mad Iris has been kidnapped just when we need her most." The frown vanished and he smiled. "Who would want to do that?" he asked.

"Who?" demanded Mrs Norton. "We don't know. Do you?"

"I think I have a pretty good idea," said Ross.

"Stop messing about and tell us then!" shouted the others.

Ross smiled again. "Top End Primary, of course. It's just the sort of nasty trick they would pull. They've stolen Mad Iris to make sure that we play badly on Friday."

Mr Grimble looked at Mrs Norton. "He could be right," he nodded.

Mrs Norton looked at Buster. "He could be right," she agreed.

Buster looked at Katie. "He could be right," he said.

Katie beamed a big smile at Ross. "You are so clever. I always knew you were brainy as well as good looking."

"Oooh!" said Mrs Norton, with a twinkle in her eye. "Who's a lucky boy?"

Ross stopped smiling. He scowled instead, and while he scowled his face turned very, very red. Because secretly he was very, very pleased!

Mr Grimble stamped back to his office. "I am going to speak to the head teacher of Top End Primary. I am going to ring her up right now and ask for our ostrich back."

# Chapter 3
# Trouble at Top End Primary

The head teacher of Top End Primary School was called Miss Sly. When Mr Grimble rang she was having a hard time. This was because Mad Iris was in her office. The ostrich liked telephones. She liked to stick them into interesting places, like cups of coffee.

But the thing that Iris liked best was to pick the telephone up and bang it on hard

things like table tops and Miss Sly's head. Miss Sly's head made lovely noises when Mad Iris hit it with a telephone. It went "OW!" and "STOPPITT!"

All this made life very difficult for Miss Sly. It was hard to have a proper talk with Mr Grimble. "Why on earth would we want to steal your ostrich, Mr Grimble?" she snapped, as she tried to stop Iris from grabbing the phone.

"Because you want to stop us from winning the football cup on Friday," said Mr Grimble.

"You're being ridiculous," hissed Miss Sly. "*Gerroff!*" She waved a frantic hand at Mad Iris, so the ostrich pecked it. "Ow!" Then Mad Iris grabbed the phone in her beak and shook it hard to see if it rattled. It didn't. How boring. Iris decided to hide the phone. She stuffed it inside Miss Sly's shirt.

"Wargh! Argh!" screamed Miss Sly. The school secretary hurried into Miss Sly's office. She screamed too. The school secretary wasn't being attacked or anything. She just *liked* screaming.

"Aargh!"

So now they were both screaming and Iris thought it was wonderful. The ostrich got rather over-excited and decided to chase Miss Sly and her secretary up and down the corridor for a bit.

At the other end of the line Mr Grimble listened to the screams. He smiled and put down his phone. Only one thing could cause so much trouble – Mad Iris. Now he was quite sure that Top End Primary had kidnapped the ostrich.

But how on earth could Pudding Lane get their mascot back?

"We should go straight over there and get her," said Mrs Norton.

Mr Grimble shook his head. "We can't just march into someone else's school and ask for our ostrich back. They'll call the police and we might get arrested. Anyway, I expect they'll hide Mad Iris somewhere until the match is over and done with."

The two teachers looked at each other and they both gave a long sigh. They couldn't think what to do.

# Chapter 4
# Who is Monstermash?

Mr Grimble and Mrs Norton couldn't think of a plan to rescue Mad Iris. So that left everything up to Ross and his class. They talked about it all through break time. Ian Tufnell, who was a big boy and a judo expert, came up with an idea.

"Let's burst into Top End Primary and grab her," he suggested, with a war-like glint in his eyes.

"The teachers will stop us," Katie pointed out.

"No, they won't. We'll tie them to their chairs."

Katie sighed. "Ian, there are lots more of them than there are of us. They'll overpower us. If anyone gets tied to chairs, it will be us!"

"She's right," Buster nodded.

"No way," said Ian. "I can do judo. They'll never tie me down."

"Yeah? Well, I can do origami," said Ross, and he winked at Katie.

Katie started to laugh. "Origami's paper-folding!" she said. "How's that going to help?"

"It'll give them a surprise," chuckled

Ross. "And while the teachers are being surprised by my origami skills, you can rescue Mad Iris."

Ian Tufnell stared at Katie and Ross moodily. He couldn't see what was funny at all. "You're stupid," he muttered.

"Yeah, and so is trying to beat up all the teachers at Top End Primary with judo," Ross pointed out.

"So what's your plan then, clever clogs?" asked Ian.

Ross and Katie looked at each other. No, they didn't have a plan. "Idiots," growled Ian, and he slunk off.

Katie waited until Ian was out of the way. Then she told Ross and Buster that, in fact, she *did* have a plan. "We'll have to break into the school and rescue Iris. We could do it in the middle of the night."

Buster didn't think this idea would work. "The school will have loads of alarms. We'll never get in without setting them off."

"Suppose we did it really quickly? Maybe we could get in and out before the police arrive," said Ross. But Buster shook his head again. It was too risky.

Katie suddenly grabbed their arms. Her eyes shone. "How about we just walk in? We go in like everyone else, at the beginning of the day. If we wear the Top End school uniform nobody will notice us."

"Where are we going to get Top End uniforms from?" asked Ross.

Katie was almost jumping up and down with excitement. "That boy next door to you! He goes to Top End. His mum washes his uniform and hangs it on the line in the back garden to dry. All you have to do is nip over the fence and nick it!"

Ross suddenly understood Katie's plan. And he saw the whole horror of it. You see, Katie was right. His next door neighbour did go to Top End, but Katie had left out something very important.

"That boy next door is called Monstermash," Ross groaned.

"Why?" asked Buster.

"Because he's a monster and he mashes people," Ross replied. "So now I have to steal a school uniform from a maniac, get into Top End school, find Mad Iris and rescue her. I am going to get totally murdered." Ross sat down and sighed. "Great."

Katie stroked his arm and smiled. "Don't worry," she said. "I'll kiss it better for you."

"Oh double great," said Ross, with an even bigger sigh.

# Chapter 5

# Watch Out for Custard Man!

Meanwhile, in Top End Primary, Mad Iris had decided that this school was not nearly as much fun as Pudding Lane. She had also decided that if Top End wasn't going to make any fun for her, then she would have to make fun for them.

The first thing she did was to take assembly. As you probably know, ostriches are not supposed to take assembly.

However, Mad Iris was a very special ostrich. She waited until Miss Sly was standing in front of all the children. Then Iris took control.

"Please stand," said Miss Sly to the children. "We will now sing *Morning has* ... waaaaargh!" Iris's head had suddenly popped up behind Miss Sly. Iris grabbed the song book from her and threw it at the front row.

"I'll save you!" cried Mr Dubbin, the deputy head. He jumped up and ran over to Iris. Somehow he landed on top of her back. Mad Iris took off at once, with Mr Dubbin clinging to her neck.

Off she went, racing away down the corridor. SPLIP! SPLAP! went her enormous feet as she raced off.

"Help!" yelled Mr Dubbin. "I'm being kidnapped by an ostrich!"

Iris dashed into the school kitchen and the cooks began screaming. "Help! Alien invaders from Mars!" they shouted. They dropped all their pots and pans. Iris didn't like that horrible noise. She did what ostriches do when they are scared. She hid her head. She stuffed her head into a giant bowl of cold custard so that she couldn't hear anything.

It was bad luck that Mr Dubbin was still clinging to her back. He slid down her thin, scrawny neck, hit the edge of the custard bowl and then fell on the floor. The custard bowl wobbled for a moment and then tipped all its contents over Mr Dubbin's head. Even Mad Iris was surprised. Where had the custard bowl gone? A minute ago she had felt safe, her head hidden inside it.

"You useless idiots!" cried the cooks. "You've ruined the pudding now! Get out!" They picked up their egg whisks and big wooden spoons and chased Mr Dubbin and Iris back out into the corridor.

Mad Iris went splatting back to the hall, shaking the custard from her head. Behind her was Mr Dubbin. And behind him were three very cross cooks.

All of them burst into the hall, where Miss Sly was trying to calm all the children down. Now they all began screaming again. A sloppy, yellow monster was on the loose! And a mad ostrich! Teachers and children scattered in all directions. Some climbed up the wallbars in the hall. Some hid behind chairs.

Poor Mr Dubbin could hardly see where he was going because his eyes were full of

custard. (So were his ears and nose and just about every other part of him.) He kept bumping into people.

Mad Iris was still trying to get away from all the noise. At last she found a small, quiet room with nobody in it. It was the library. Iris peered at all the books. They looked very nice. Would they taste nice too? She ate one, and it did. So she ate another.

Miss Sly was in the corridor outside the little library. She crept towards the door. BANG!! She slammed it shut. Mad Iris was a prisoner. Miss Sly gave a big sigh of relief. At last everyone was safe.

Suddenly there was a terrible noise from the far end of the corridor. A sloppy, yellow maniac came charging towards her. Behind the madman were three cooks, hurling plates and spoons and forks at him now.

"STOP THIS NONSENSE AT ONCE!" roared Miss Sly. Then she was hit by a flying saucer (a real flying saucer!). She crumpled into a heap on the floor.

So that was the end of assembly at Top End Primary.

# Chapter 6
# Ross Gets Brave

In an odd way Iris had already done something that was going to help Ross a lot. Half the children from Top End School went home splattered with custard. Monstermash was one of them. His mum made him take off his uniform at once. It went straight into the washing machine. An hour later it was hanging out to dry on the line in the garden.

Ross waited until it was getting dark. He knew that Monstermash's mum would take the uniform back indoors very soon. He had to get into the garden next door and grab it.

"OK," he said to himself. "I have got to do this. I shall count to three. One, two,

three …" Ross bit his lip. It was no good. He couldn't do it. He stayed in his own garden.

"I must be brave," he told himself. "I'll count to three, and then I'll do the final countdown, and then I'll do it. Right. Here we go. One, two, three … and final countdown … three, two, one, a half, a quarter, er … ZERO! GO! GO! GO!"

Ross jumped up onto the fence and dropped down into next door's garden. He raced across the grass. He grabbed the sweatshirt, pulled the trousers off the line and dashed back. He was back over the fence again in one jump and he did three victory laps round his own garden.

"I am the champion!" he yelled. Then he had to hide behind the shed as Monstermash's mum came into the garden and began to take in the washing. She frowned. She scowled. She looked all around. Something was missing. She shook her head a few times and went back inside.

Ross grinned. He stuffed the uniform up his jumper and sneaked back indoors. His heart was still thumping like all of the drums in a drum kit, but he felt fantastic. He'd done it! All he had to do now was walk into Top End Primary the next morning.

Aaaaaaaaaaaaarrrgh!!!

Ross turned white from top to toe. *What was he saying?* Did he really think he could get away with it? Was he mad? Was he crazy? Would he get killed a hundred times over? Probably.

GULP!

# Chapter 7
# Ross Gets even Braver

The next morning was Friday morning. It was the day of the football final. Ross and Katie stood at the corner of the street next to Top End Primary and watched the children going into school.

"They look very big," said Ross.

"You'll be fine," said Katie.

"I look like an idiot in this uniform," Ross pointed out.

It was true. He *did* look like an idiot. Monstermash was much bigger then Ross. Some people might even say that Monstermash was *too* big. They just wouldn't say it when Monstermash was listening. The trousers were too long and they were much too big round the middle. The sweatshirt was too large and the sleeves dangled a long way past Ross's hands.

"I'm going to get killed," said Ross.

"No, you're not. You're going to go into the school. You're going to find Iris and you're going to rescue her. Then you'll be a great hero and you'll be able to marry the princess, just like a fairy tale."

Ross scowled. "I suppose you're the princess?" Katie beamed up at him and nodded. Ross sighed. "I'd better get going," he said.

"Good luck," whispered Katie, blowing him a kiss.

Ross turned very red and shuffled towards the school entrance. At any moment he thought someone was going to grab him and say, "Hey! You're not from our school!" But he got through the front gate without anyone saying a word. He got through the front door and still nobody stopped him. All of a sudden Ross began to think that he might just be able to do this amazing thing. He might find Iris. He might rescue her. He might become a hero – a real hero! He might marry the princess! Noooooo! Nightmare!!! He didn't want to marry any princesses!!

"Hey! You boy!" Ross stopped and swung round. He found himself face to face with Miss Sly, the headteacher. She had a plaster above her eye where she'd been hit by a flying saucer the day before. It made her look a bit like a pirate. She was scary!

"Where are you going? You know the classrooms are back that way. Whose class are you in?"

Ross was in a panic. He didn't know the name of any of the teachers at Top End. Then, as he was trying to think of what to say, Miss Sly peered closely at him.

"Are those your trousers? They look awfully big."

"They're my brother's," Ross said quickly. "I wet mine." Ross gritted his teeth. How could he say such a stupid thing?

"You WET your trousers?"

"I mean I spilled my drink on them," Ross said fast. "This morning. At breakfast. Milk."

Miss Sly shook her head. "You're a strange boy. Well, don't just stand there pulling faces at me and looking like a prize fool. Get to your class."

Ross turned away and hurried back down the corridor. Phew! A narrow escape. As he walked he looked into the rooms on both sides. And there she was! Mad Iris! She was in the ... well, what room could it be? Ross thought it had probably been the library once. Before Mad Iris came.

Mad Iris had grabbed every single book. She'd pecked them and kicked them. She'd thrown them at the windows. She'd thrown them at the walls and ceiling. She'd played football with them. In fact, Iris had done just about everything she could do to them, except read them.

Ross checked that nobody was looking and slipped into the room. Mad Iris was so pleased to see someone she knew. She liked Ross. Ross was fun. She went straight across to him and tried to pull all his hair out.

"Stop it!" hissed Ross. "Don't worry. I've come to rescue you. We're going to escape."

Mad Iris picked up what was left of a book about Vikings and tried to stuff it down the back of Ross's sweatshirt. He swung round and grabbed it from her. "Stop it! Behave yourself."

Ross poked his head round the door. His heart was beating like a drum kit again. He and Mad Iris had to make their escape *now*.

"Follow me," he whispered to the ostrich. "Don't make a sound."

# Chapter 8

## Ross Gets his Bravery Reward

"Come on," said Ross. "Keep very quiet."
Iris and Ross stepped into the corridor.
BANG!

What on earth made that noise? It was
Mad Iris. She was stuck in the doorway. She
had a chair in her beak and she was trying
to take it out of the library with her. Ross
pushed her quickly back into the room and

took the chair away. "I told you to behave," he said sternly. "Now, let's try again."

This time they got into the corridor without any trouble. At the end of the corridor was the front entrance and beyond that – freedom. Ross kept his eyes on the front entrance and marched towards it. Just then a classroom door opened and out came a boy. Monstermash!

Monstermash stood right in front of Ross and stared at him. Ross was sure Monstermash would know who he was. Wasn't Ross his next door neighbour, after all?

"Don't I ...?" began Monstermash.

"No, you don't," said Ross firmly, and shook his head. But Monstermash went on staring and staring at him. He stood right in front of Ross, blocking the corridor. Ross couldn't move.

"Aren't you …?"

"No, I'm not," said Ross, even more firmly. Now Monstermash peered at Ross's clothes.

"Aren't those …?"

"No, they aren't," said Ross quickly. "Well, I must get going. Got to take the ostrich to the vet. She's having her toenails clipped."

Monstermash looked down at Iris's horny feet. She did have very long toenails. He moved to one side. Ross pulled Iris after him and headed on down the corridor. A few moments later he was pushing the front door open and then they were outside. Freedom!

Ross almost ran down the school path but he kept his cool just long enough. But when Mad Iris saw Katie the ostrich began to gallop towards her. Katie threw her arms round the ostrich's neck.

"Oh, Iris," she sighed, "it's so good to see you." Mad Iris was pleased to see Katie too so she ate Katie's tie. Well, she tried, but it was still attached to Katie's neck, which made things tricky for both of them.

"I did it!" said Ross. "I did it!"

"My hero!" smiled Katie, kissing Ross on the cheek.

"Urgh!" went Ross. After all the dangers he'd been through he'd been got in the end!

# Chapter 9
# The Football Final

The football final was held at Pudding Lane. Mr Grimble had kept Mad Iris hidden until the match started. "She'll be a surprise," he said.

Katie and the Pudding Lane team were shocked when they saw how big the Top End players were. They looked enormous and they stood in a row, grinning like tigers at the Pudding Lane team.

"We're going to get killed," muttered Buster. "What kind of flowers would you like on your grave?"

"Poppies," whispered Katie, and the match began.

In fact, Top End were not very good at football. But they were very clever at fouling without being caught. They tried every trick in the book. It wasn't long before Top End had scored three goals and Pudding Lane were three-nil down.

That was the moment that Mr Grimble decided to bring Mad Iris out. He paraded her round the pitch. A great cheer went up from Pudding Lane and the ostrich strutted up and down, eyeing the ball. That football was the most interesting thing Iris had seen for ages. She did a little dance, pounding the earth with her feet, as if she were getting ready for a penalty kick.

As soon as they saw Mad Iris, the Pudding Lane players got a new burst of life. Moments later Katie and Buster both scored goals. The score was 3-2. Top End were furious. Monstermash fouled Buster. He hacked him so hard, Buster was put out of the game. He had to be carried off on a stretcher.

Once again Top End was winning and they scored again. But Katie wasn't giving up and minutes later she scored Pudding Lane's third goal.

Monstermash was furious. "Girls shouldn't play football," he hissed, and he stamped on Katie's foot. Hard.

"Argh!" Katie crashed to the ground. She hugged her injured ankle. It hurt.

"You can't do that!" Ross yelled angrily. But the ref hadn't seen anything wrong.

"Oh, I am SO sorry," smirked Monstermash. "Did I hurt the little girlie?" he added in a whisper.

Ross helped Katie as she limped to the side. She was out of the game and now Pudding Lane were down to nine players. After that it was a romp for Top End. They scored again and again. Mr Grimble couldn't bear to watch any longer. Neither could the rest of the school and some of them began to drift away from the game. Ross was so angry he didn't know what to do.

But Mad Iris did. She marched onto the pitch and went straight for that wonderful black and white ball. She kicked it. She pushed it with her beak. She raced upfield and BANG!

"Goal!" yelled Ross.

"She can't play!" yelled the Top End players. "She's an ostrich! Hey, ref – get that ostrich sent off."

But the ref couldn't send Mad Iris off the pitch. There was nothing in the rules to say that ostriches couldn't play football. Ross said that Iris was a substitute for the two injured players. The ref smiled to himself. He was quite happy with that and the game went on.

It wasn't long before the score was ten-all. There was only one minute of play left. Someone kicked the ball way up into the air. Up and up it went. Everyone rushed towards it, but Mad Iris was ahead of them.

She bustled past them all and with one great jump she soared up into the air and BAM! Mad Iris headed the ball so hard it almost knocked the goalkeeper's head off. The ball shot straight into the back of the net.

The referee blew his whistle and that was it – victory for Pudding Lane! 11-10 to them!

The school had never seen such a fantastic parade. Everyone was cheering, even the caretaker and the cook.

Miss Sly had to hand over the football cup to Mr Grimble. He wasn't quick enough. Mad Iris grabbed it first and went scampering round and round the school with it. She had decided that the cup was

hers, and she was right really. After all, she'd scored the winning goal.

"How's your foot?" Ross asked Katie.

"It's a bit sore," she answered. She was holding an ice pack on it. She gave Ross a winning smile and lifted off the ice pack. "It just needs to be kissed better," she said.

Ross turned white. He would do almost anything for Katie. He had pinched a school uniform from right under Monstermash's nose. He had walked into Top End Primary and rescued Mad Iris. He had faced almost certain death! But there had to be limits. No way was he going to KISS KATIE'S FOOT!

Barrington Stoke would like to thank all its readers for commenting on the manuscript before publication and in particular:

Akash Abraham

Christopher Adams

Joseph Andrews

Aaron Bamford

Reece Bayne

Kayleigh Beattie

Stephen Bodily

Robyn Bradley

Ross Bruchlowsky

Chloe Budd

Lewis Butcher

Ellie Louise Buttrick

Rachel Christian

Mrs J Clark

Ben Clarkson

Mrs Colquhoun

Joe Cooke

Ben Deabill

Jade Dilley

Louis Ellison

Sophie Felton

Caitlin Foster

Sophie Fowkes

Tamara Gayle

Michael H

Aaron Harrison

Charlotte Hemus

Zack Hendry

Harriet Henshaw-Bancroft

Chris Holyroyd

Dennie Hunter

Christopher Hurlstone

## Become a Consultant!

Would you like to give us feedback on our titles before they are published? Contact us at the email address below – we'd love to hear from you!

info@barringtonstoke.co.uk
www.barringtonstoke.co.uk

Barrington Stoke would like to thank all its readers for commenting on the manuscript before publication and in particular:

| | |
|---|---|
| Ross Huskisson | Amy Randall |
| Charlie Inger | Daniel Randall |
| Daniel Johnson | Conor Reeve |
| Bronwen Kearney | Payge Riley |
| Cameron Lander | Christopher Robinson |
| Francesca Mabe | April Simmons |
| Daniel Marriott | Shannon Smith |
| Joey Mburu-Newman | Joseph Steeples |
| Holly McLaughlin | Jack Stuckey |
| Sureka Mehmi | Cameron Thurgood |
| Marion Milroy | Hal & Max Travers |
| Shane Nicholls | Travis Tulloch-Darroux |
| Elizabeth Pacey | Jack Turner |
| Clara Pennock | Jack Whetstone |
| Oscar Hendry Pickup | Sophie Wing |
| Rebecca Potter | Robbie Woolgar |

## Become a Consultant!

Would you like to give us feedback on our titles before they are published? Contact us at the email address below – we'd love to hear from you!

info@barringtonstoke.co.uk
www.barringtonstoke.co.uk

# If you loved this, why don't you try ...

# Mad Iris
# by Jeremy Strong

Would you like to have an ostrich for a pet? Ross has big problems when one turns up in the school playground. How can he save her from the men in black who want to kill her? And why is Katie stuck in the boys' toilets?

**You can order *Mad Iris* directly from our website at www.barringtonstoke.co.uk**